queen bee

This book belongs to

....

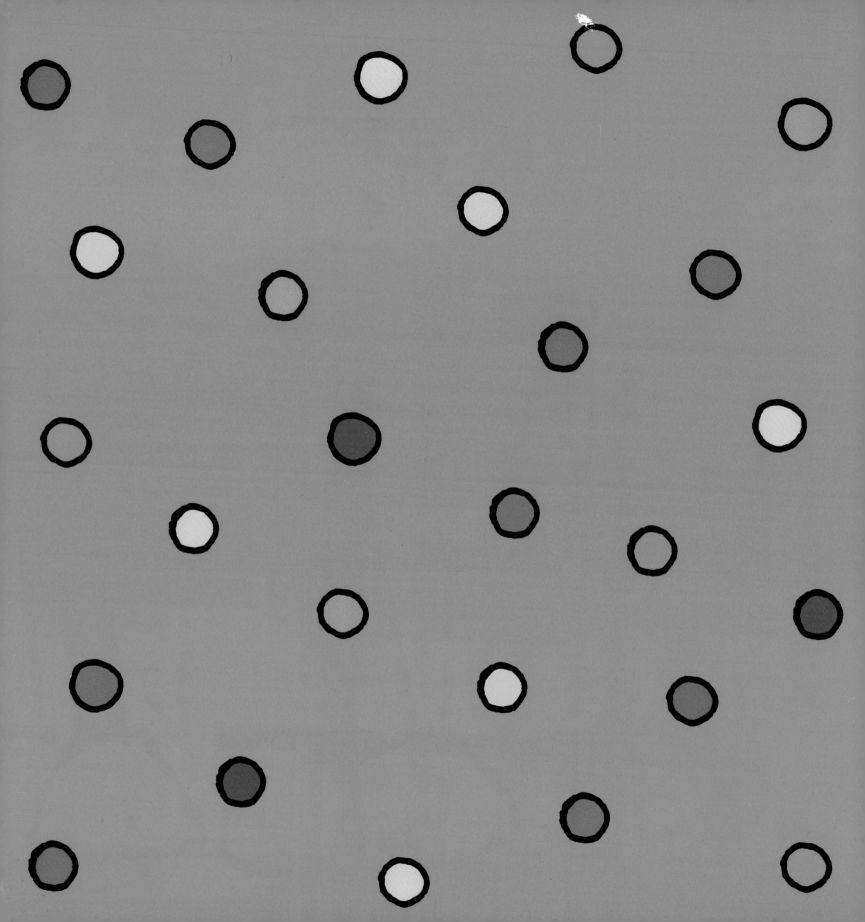

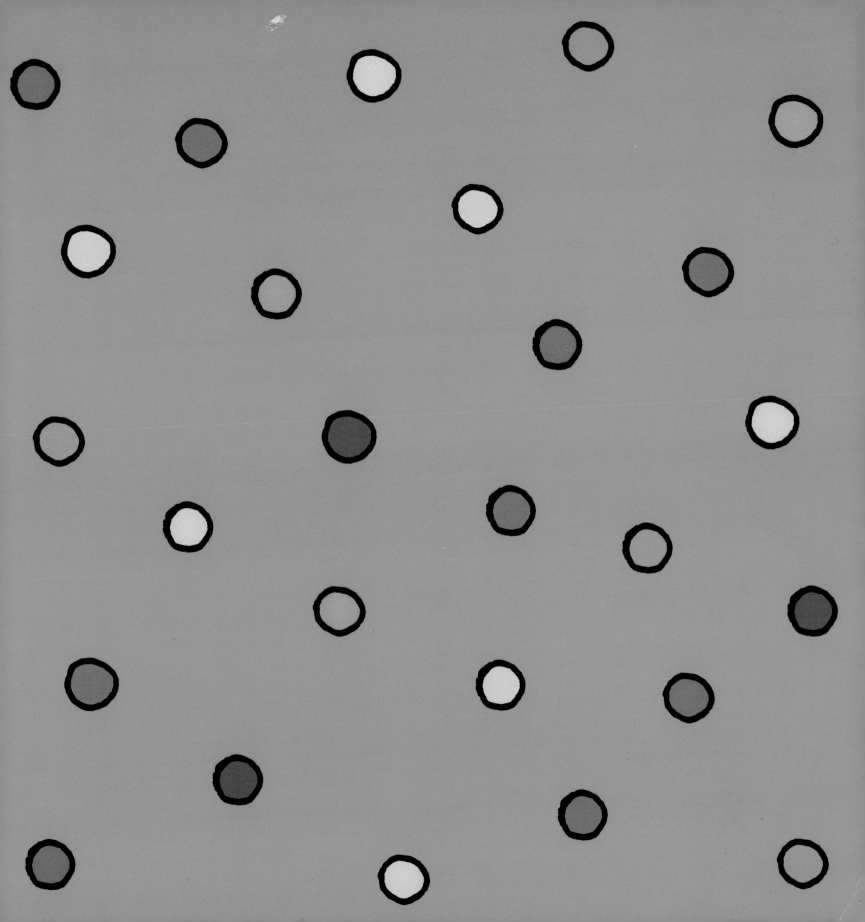

how many spots,
triceratops?

Can you count your spots, triceratops?

Yes, and I can count...

one
horn on unicorn

two
twitchy
hoppity
rabbits

2

3

three
jewels on queen bee's crown

four
blue shoes on horse's feet

4

five
wobbly legs on jellyfish

5

6

six
spiky whiskers
on cat

8

eight
dangly legs
on spider

and **nine** slimy snails

all in a line

9

But how many spots have YOU got, triceratops?

ten!
no one has more spots than me

I do!

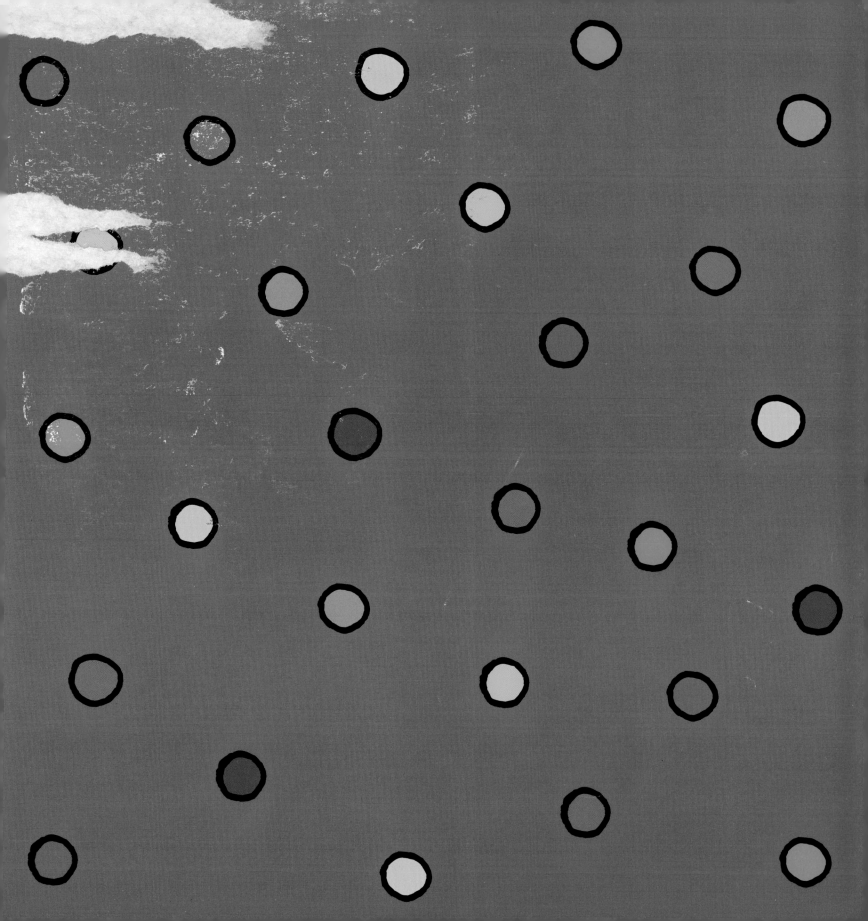

bang on the door ™ ©

OXFORD
UNIVERSITY PRESS

Great Clarendon Street, Oxford OX2 6DP

Oxford   New York

Auckland Bangkok Buenos Aires Cape Town Chennai Dar es Salaam Delhi Hong Kong
Istanbul Karachi Kolkata Kuala Lumpur Madrid Melbourne Mexico City Mumbai
Nairobi São Paulo Shanghai Taipei Tokyo Toronto

Oxford is a registered trade mark of Oxford University Press
in the UK and in certain other countries

Bang on the door character copyright: © 2003 Bang on the Door all rights reserved

bang on the door ™ © is a trade mark

Exclusive right to license by Santoro

Text © Oxford University Press 2003

www.bangonthedoor.com

The moral rights of the author and artists have been asserted

Database right Oxford University Press (maker)

First published 2003

All rights reserved.

British Library Cataloguing in Publication Data available

ISBN 0-19-272556-4 (paperback)

1 3 5 7 9 10 8 6 4 2

Typeset in Freeflow

Printed in China